Tiptoe Joe

By Ginger Foglesong Gibson

ILLUSTRATED BY Laura Rankin

Greenwillow Books
An Imprint of HarperCollinsPublishers

Tiptoe Joe

Text copyright © 2013 by Ginger Foglesong Gibson; illustrations copyright © 2013 by Laura Rankin.
All rights reserved. Manufactured in China. For information address HarperCollins Children's Books,
a division of HarperCollins Publishers,
10 East 53rd Street, New York, NY 10022. www.harpercollinschildrens.com

Watercolors were used to prepare the full-color art.
The text type is Weiss Medium.

Library of Congress Cataloging-in-Publication Data

Gibson, Ginger Foglesong.
Tiptoe Joe / by Ginger Foglesong Gibson ; illustrated by Laura Rankin.
p. cm.
"Greenwillow Books"
Summary: A bear invites all of the animals to follow him through the trees,
on tiptoe, to see a special surprise.
ISBN 978-0-06-177203-0 (trade ed.)
[1. Stories in rhyme. 2. Animals—Fiction. 3. Noise—Fiction.] I. Rankin, Laura, ill. II. Title.
PZ8.3.G3586Tip 2013 [E]—dc23 2012010586

13 14 15 16 17 SCP 10 9 8 7 6 5 4 3 2 1

First Edition

 Greenwillow Books

For Gordie and Maggie
—G. F. G.

For my dad, who was *top drawer*
and *first cabin* all the way
—L. R.

Tiptoe fast,

tiptoe slow.

Say hello to Tiptoe Joe.

Donkey, Donkey, come with me.
I know something you should see.

CLOP, CLOP.

Rabbit, Rabbit, come with me.
I know something you should see.

THUMP, THUMP.

Turkey, Turkey, come with me.
I know something you should see.

Tell us, tell us, Tiptoe Joe.
What's the secret? Let us know.

FLAP, FLAP. THUMP, THUMP. CLOP, CLOP.

Tiptoe, tiptoe, quiet please.

Tiptoe underneath the trees.

Moose, Moose, come with me.
I know something you should see.

THUD,

THUD.

Owl, Owl, come with me.
I know something you should see.

Beaver, Beaver, come with me.
I know something you should see.

SLAP,

SLAP.

Tell us, tell us, Tiptoe Joe.
What's the secret? Let us know.

SWISH,
SWISH.

SLAP,
SLAP.

THUD,
THUD.

Tiptoe, tiptoe, quiet please.
Tiptoe underneath the trees.

THUD, THUD.

SWISH, SWISH.

FLAP, FLAP.

SLAP, SLAP.

Tiptoe lightly.
Point your toe.

THUD,
THUD.

SWISH,
SWISH.

SLAP,
SLAP.

Tell us, tell us, Tiptoe Joe.
What's the secret? Let us know.

Tiptoe, tiptoe,
softly creep.

Here's my secret, fast asleep.